This book belongs to

Neve Donohoe

Doodelicious!

An Hachette UK Company
www.hachette.co.uk

First published in the USA in 2015 by Ticktock,
an imprint of Octopus Publishing Group Ltd
Endeavour House
189 Shaftesbury Avenue
London
WC2H 8JY
www.octopusbooks.co.uk
www.octopusbooksusa.com
www.ticktockbooks.com

Copyright © Octopus Publishing Group Ltd 2015

Distributed in the US by
Hachette Book Group USA
1290 Avenue of the Americas
4th and 5th Floors
New York, NY 10020

Distributed in Canada by
Canadian Manda Group
664 Annette Street
Toronto, Ontario,
Canada M6S 2C8

ISBN 978-1-78325-263-3

Printed and bound in China
10 9 8 7 6 5 4 3 2 1

Series Editor: Anna Bowles
Design: Andy Archer
Creative Director: Miranda Snow
Managing Editor: Karen Rigden
Production Controller: Sarah-Jayne Johnson

Image sources: Shutterstock; 123RF; YAY Images; Thinkstock

Draw and create your own

CARTOONS
&
MANGA

Ticktock

CARTOON EYES

The eyes are very important when you're drawing a cartoon character as they show emotion, but they don't need to be complicated.

Practice drawing eyes like these.

EYES

To create angry eyes, draw the eyebrows pointing downwards, towards the nose. The pupils are positioned at the top of the eyes.

If you color the eyeball red then the character will look very angry indeed!

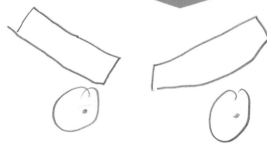

Practice drawing some angry eyes.

EYES

To create happy eyes, draw round pupils. The eyebrows are raised slightly above the eyes and the pupils are positioned in their centers.

Practice drawing some happy eyes.

To create surprised eyes, draw them round or oval. The eyebrows are raised high above the eyes and the pupils can be positioned anywhere.

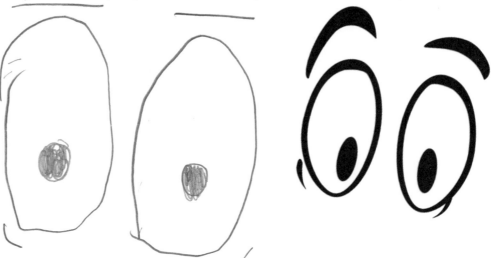

Really surprised eyes can be drawn popping out!

Practice drawing some surprised eyes.

EYES

Here are some examples of eyes showing different emotions.

Now you can try drawing some more eyes. How about drawing eyes that look worried, romantic or greedy?

EYES

It often looks good if the eyes are very close together or even overlapping.

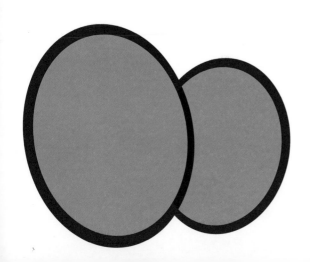

Practice drawing more eyes here.

EYES

The two eyes don't always have to look exactly the same.

Try to draw an odd-looking pair of eyes.

MANGA EYES

Eyes in manga are the most important feature, so you need to practice, practice, **practice!**

Here are some more manga eyes to practice.
These are boys' eyes, so don't include long eyelashes.

EYES

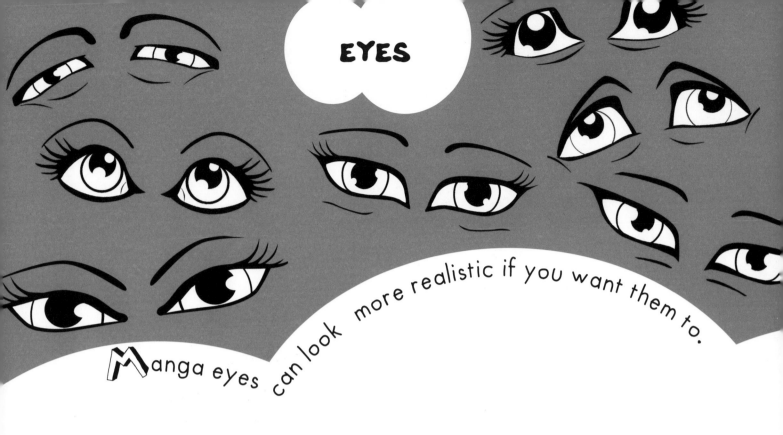

EYES

Manga eyes can look more realistic if you want them to.

Draw the other eye to make a pair.

Look out for drawings of eyes in magazines and comics. Cut out the ones you like and glue them here so that you can copy this style.

Practice drawing the eyes you like the most from the pictures you have collected.

GLASSES

Glasses can be any shape you like.

Why not draw some eyes in these glasses?

Add glasses and other features to turn these shapes into cartoon characters.

Cut out pictures of glasses and keep them to help you draw and design glasses for your cartoon characters.

Practice drawing glasses you like from the pictures you have collected.

You can make a cartoon character based on a ball.

Here's baseball guy!

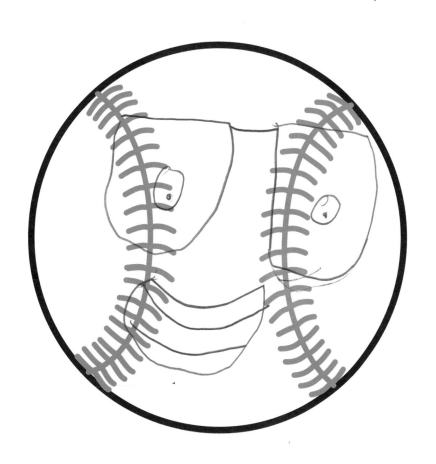

Create your own baseball character.

Now try to create a tennis ball character.

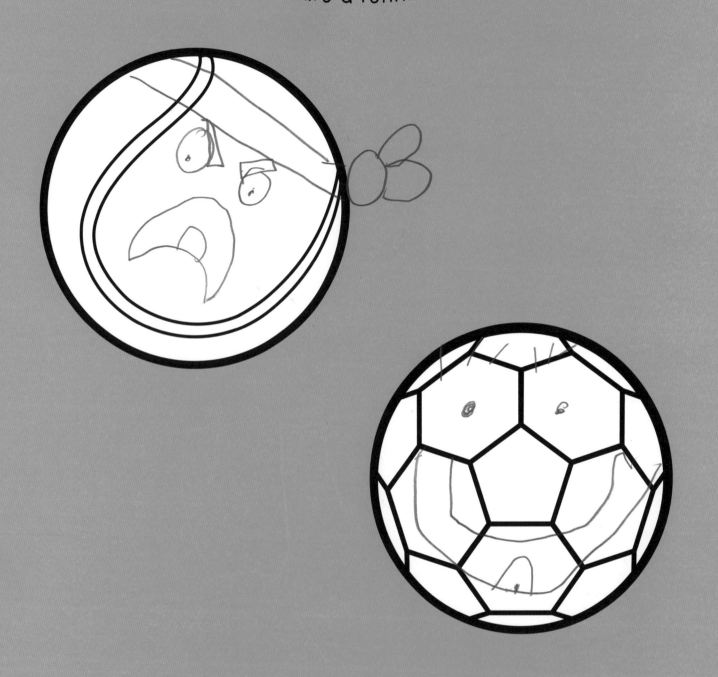

Will your soccer character be wearing soccer boots or high heels?

Even an ice-cream can become a cartoon character.

Create an ice-cream family!

CHARACTERS

Look around the kitchen for vegetables to inspire more characters. Draw your vegetable people here.

These are some more ideas.

Add legs and arms to these vegetables.

Will they be wearing shoes, boots or gloves?

Are they happy, goofy or hopping mad?

CHARACTERS

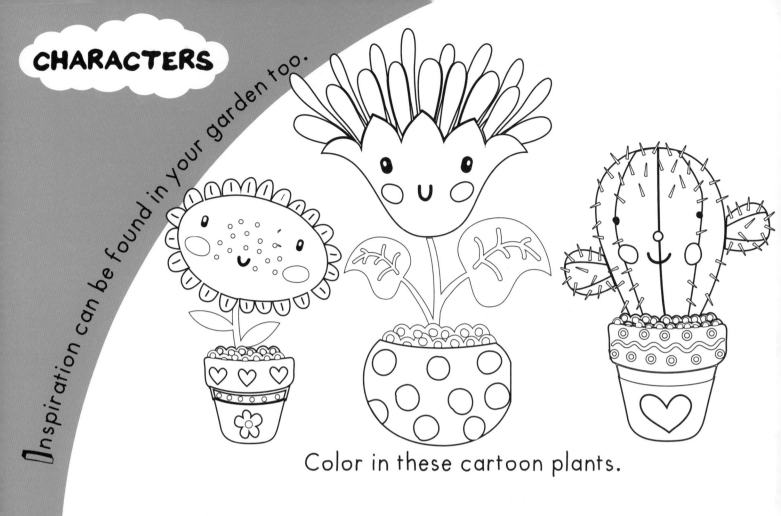

Color in these cartoon plants.

Add three cartoon plants to these pots.

You can create manga-style anything. Just use your imagination. Color these weird creatures in, then create one of your own.

FINGERPRINT CARTOONS

Use an ink pad or paint to make fingerprints.
Add legs and arms to turn them into fingerprint people.

Will you add hair, hats or horns?

CARTOON FACES

Draw around something circular.

A large round coin is great to use.

Practice smiley faces. Remember: as the smile gets bigger the cheeks push up and cover the lower part of the eyes.

MOUTHS

Mouths can be a simple line, or more complicated.

Practice drawing these mouths.

Look in magazines and comics for good cartoon mouths.
Cut them out and glue them here.

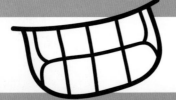

Practice drawing the mouths you like the most from the pictures you have collected.

NOSES

Noses can be more expressive than you might think. Check out these pudgy, pointy and even warty noses.

Practice drawing different noses.

Then you can mix things up. Add a pig's nose to a cat. Or add a clown's nose to a banana. What else can you think of?

MOUSTACHES

And under the nose, a moustache can often be found.

Add a moustache to each animal. You can make them as wacky as you wish.

You can make a cartoon character from just a nose, glasses and a moustache.

Have a go at drawing some.

MONSTERS

Color in these little monsters.

Monsters often have teeth.

Practice monster teeth here.

Monsters don't have to be regular shapes.

It's a good idea to draw around objects you find in your house. Then turn those outlines into cartoon monsters.

You could draw around a key, a glove or some scissors!

Monsters can just be squares with faces.
Meet the Box Monsters!

Create your own Box Monsters.

Manga monsters don't have to be scary. Here's a very cute monster waving at you!

Using very simple shapes and curved lines,
draw and color your own cute monsters.

ROBOTS

If you put boxes of different shapes and sizes together you can create a robot.

Color in these robots.

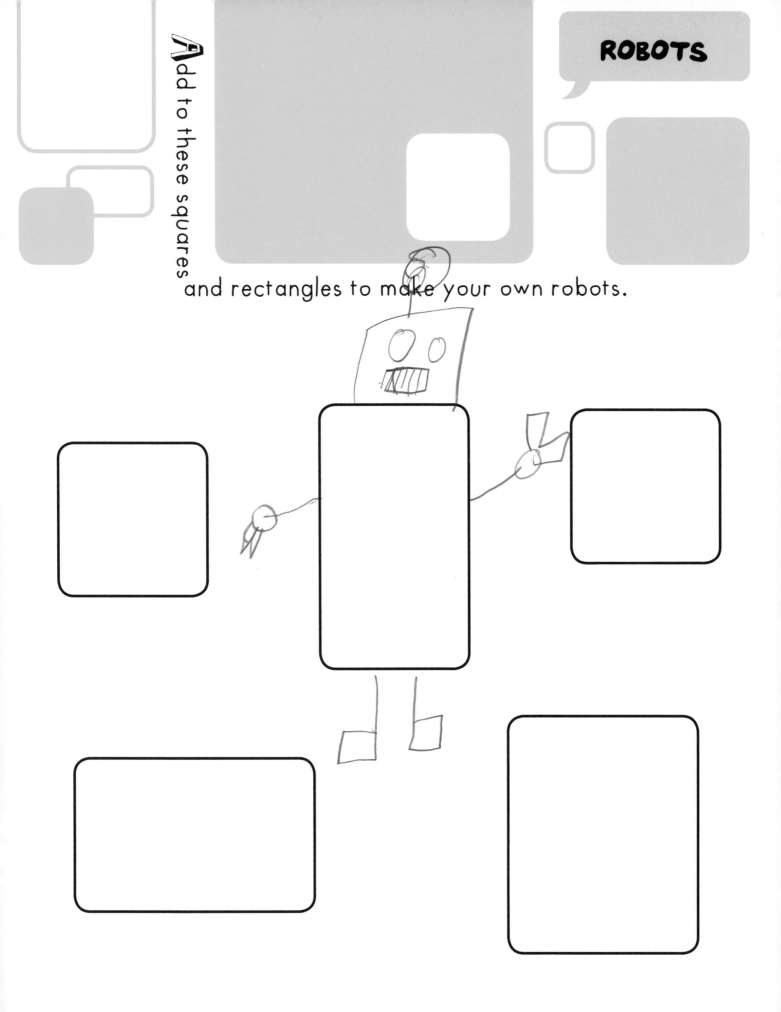

ROBOTS

Add to these squares and rectangles to make your own robots.

You could include other shapes to add more detail.

GHOSTS

Even manga ghosts can be cuddly!

Draw your own ghosts. By altering their mouths they can be happy, sad or confused.

If you want girly ghosts, add curly eyelashes.

PEOPLE

You can practice adding movement to your cartoons. It's best to do this with simple characters.

Practice drawing your own running, jumping, hopping, skipping and dancing people.

MOVEMENT

These cartoon children are doing a variety of activities.

Can you draw them doing some other things?

TALKING

Cartoons don't have to move. They can just stand and talk.

Fill in the speech bubbles and then color these characters.

Draw your own line of cartoon people. What will they be talking about?

FEET

Cartoon feet can be as simple or as complicated as you want to make them.

Practice drawing feet. Draw the other foot to make a pair.

SHOES

If you want your cartoon character to wear shoes, here are some styles for you to practice.

Cartoon hands can just be simple circles or as realistic as you wish.

HANDS

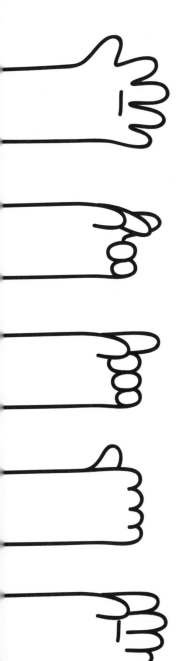

Practice different hand shapes here.

HANDS

Practice more hand shapes.

They can be clasping, pointing or just waving.

Look at your own hand to help you draw different positions.

As in real life, cartoon babies come in all shapes and sizes.

Practice drawing a baby here.

BABIES

Manga babies are super-cute!

Practice drawing this baby.

it's that simple!

If you want to create a manga boy baby don't add the bunches or hair ties – it's that simple!

These manga children look surprised, but just by altering their mouths you can make them look happy, confused or scared.

Draw your own manga children.
They could be running, jumping or sitting down.

Cartoon children can be as simple or as detailed as you wish.

A good idea is to start with a few lines. Then as you become more confident you can add more features.

Practice drawing cartoon children.

Sometimes when drawing manga children, it's fun to make their heads much bigger than their bodies.

Draw some more manga children. Don't forget the big eyes and the spiky hairstyles.

Draw your own cartoon teenagers here.

ADULTS

Adults come in all shapes and sizes too. Draw some tall and some short.

OLDIES

Don't forget old people can do adventurous things too!

People's hair, faces and posture
change as they age.

He turend old fast!

Try to draw people of different ages.

When creating a cartoon family it's best to use the same style of drawing for each person.

Create your own cartoon family.

MANGA

Here are some steps for drawing the classic female face.

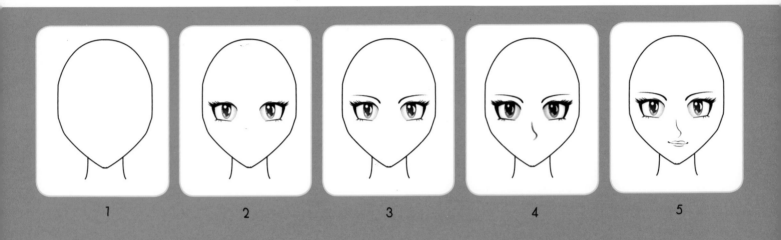

1   2   3   4   5

Finish your female face with cool spiky hair!

The male face is subtly different.

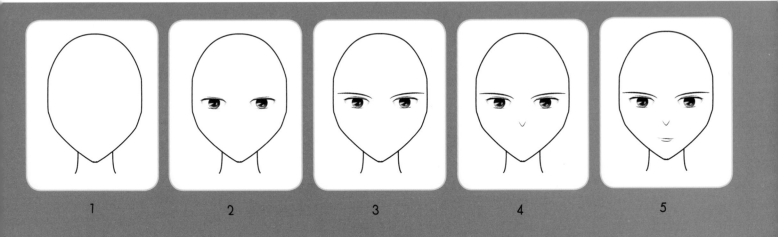

1   2   3   4   5

Manga guys have spiky hair too!

Practice tracing the heads shown here.

Manga characters have extraordinary hairstyles. Make sure you exaggerate them.

Manga boys have wacky hair, too.

BOYS' HAIR

SPEECH BUBBLES

You usually need speech bubbles to make your cartoons into a story. They can be any shape, color or size.

Color these in.

BUBBLES

Speech for cartoon characters is often written in normal handwriting. Make sure that it can be easily read!

Add words to these speech bubbles.

BUBBLES

Add words to these bubbles. Uneven bubbles are for thoughts and bubbles with a regular shape are for speech.

DINOSAURS

Cartoon dinosaurs can be friendly or scary.

Color these however you like.

DINOSAURS

There are many different ways to draw dinosaurs.

Practice drawing your style of dinosaur here.

Draw your own manga dinosaur. Remember, it's the eyes that are most important.

Add super-long eyelashes if you want to make them in to girl dinosaurs!

Color in these manga dinosaurs.

DINOSAURS

Add a few dinosaurs to this scene.

DINOSAURS

Collect pictures of your favorite dinosaurs and glue them here.

DRAGONS

Dragons can be any shape. Tall or small. Thin or round. Fierce or friendly.

Cartoon dragons can be as interesting as your imagination. Draw your dragons here.

TRANSPORT

Cartoon characters don't have to be animals or people.
They can be created from vehicles.

Try coloring these in.

Turn these vehicles into cartoon characters.

Now create your own cartoon vehicle. Will it be a rocket, a taxi or a submarine?

UNIFORMS

Different jobs need different clothing. Can you draw a cartoon character in uniform?

Make sure your character has the correct clothing and accessories.

Will you draw a fireman, a surgeon or a builder?

BACKGROUNDS

Sometimes you want your cartoon characters on a background.
Which characters will you add here?

You can always draw and cut out your cartoon characters, then glue them onto a background.

Will you add rockets and space monsters?

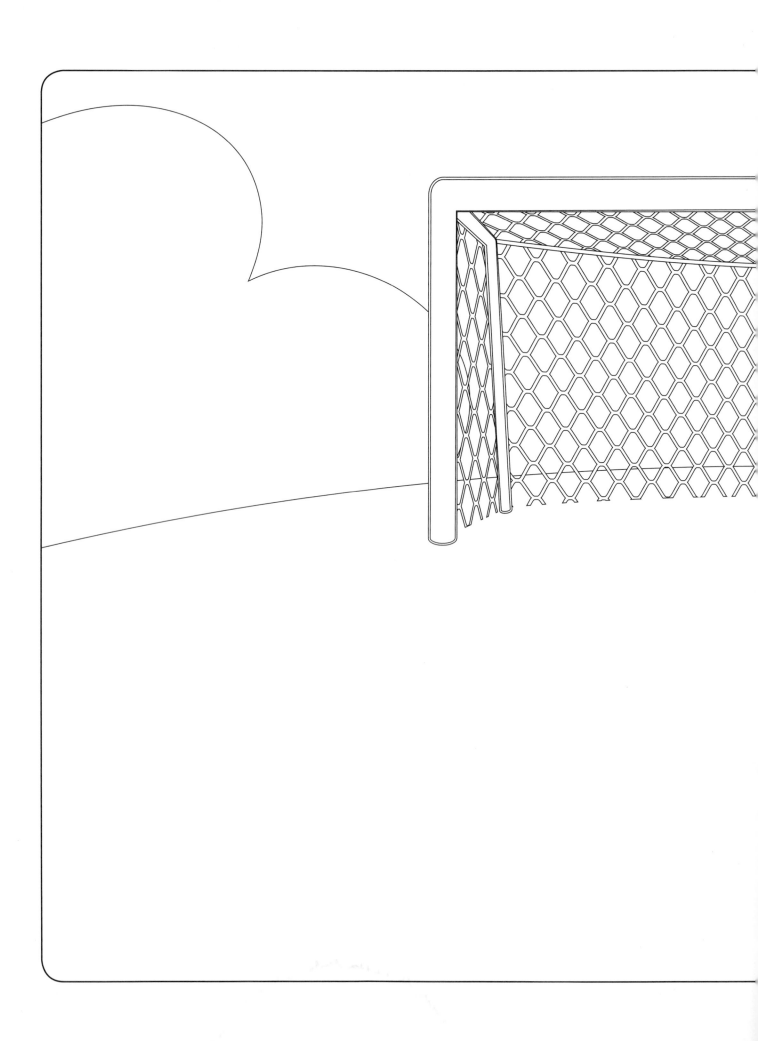

Will you add just a goalie or more players? The players could be dinos or monsters!

You can use pages from magazines and newspapers, or even sheets of wrapping paper as your background.

Color these cartoon characters, then cut them out and add them to a background.

TREES

Practice drawing a selection of different trees here.

Draw your own background, starting with trees.

When playing sports, your cartoon character will also need the correct clothing and accessories.

Create some really sporty types!

Hands and feet can be added to any object to make a cartoon character.

Choose some ordinary things to turn into cartoon characters.

You could add eyes as well.

How about a hat? Or a rain boot? Maybe a fish stick?

CARTOON ANIMALS

Animals make great cartoon characters.

Color these animals. Will you use realistic colors?

Try to find your own style of drawing. These are some cartoon pets, drawn in different styles.

Practice your style here.

MANGA ANIMALS

Manga animals are very rounded and cute.

Draw your own manga animals here.

ANIMALS

Can you create a new species?

Here's a DOGOPHANT

Combine the best parts of your favorite animals and see what you can make!

Animals don't always have to behave as you would expect them to.

Draw an animal doing something surprising!

ANIMALS

Manga animals are based on real animals. You just need to add the big manga eyes.

Draw your favorite animal in manga style!

Manga pandas are very popular, and they can be drawn in different styles.

Draw a panda. Will it be cute or fierce?

This bee is busy doing lots of different things.

Choose just one animal and draw it in as many different poses as you can.

ANIMALS

To give yourself some ideas, think about all the things that you do during the day. Then draw your cartoon animal doing them.

Manga rabbits are awesome.

Your rabbit can be as simple or as complicated as you like. Just remember to add long ears, and your drawing will look great!

Practice drawing cats. Make them as crazy as you want! How about a guitar-playing cat, a roller-skating cat or a parachuting cat?

Color these cats in bright, fun colors.

Collect pictures of your favorite cartoon animals and glue them here.

Practice drawing the ones you like the most from the pictures you've collected.

UNDER THE SEA

Color in these sea creatures. Will you choose realistic colors?

Add cartoon sea creatures to this underwater scene.
Then color it carefully.

BUILDINGS

They can be realistic, imaginary, scary or just bonkers!

Draw a range of buildings here.

BUILDINGS

POST OFFICE

HOSPITAL

SCHOOL

Can you draw an office block, a fire station and a petrol station?

COLLAGE CARTOONS

An interesting way to create cartoon characters is to cut out shapes from patterned paper or fabric to make the body or clothes, then draw the heads, legs and hands.

Try making a collage character here.

Collect patterns from your favorite comics and magazines to make more characters here.

Practice drawing the ones you like the most from the pictures you have collected.

Here are patterns to color in, then use for your collage cartoons, or as backgrounds.

Now that you're a manga and cartooning expert, it's time to start creating your own special characters. Why not draw your own cartoon family below!

Brother   Sister   Mom   Dad   Pet

USEFUL WORDS

MANGA

Anime	Japanese TV animation.
Dōjinshi	Art drawn by Japanese fans of manga or anime.
Kawaii	Cute.
Manga	Japanese comics.
Mangaka	A comic artist.
Otaku	A big fan of anime and manga.
Super-deformed	A style of art where characters are drawn very small, with stubby limbs and big heads.

COMICS

Caption	Words in a box that describe what's happening in a picture.
Colorist	A person who adds colors to comic panels.
Frame	The borders of a panel.
Graphic novel	A novel in comic-strip format.
Gutter	The space between the panels of a comic.
Inker	A person who traces over pencil lines with ink.
Layout	The way in which text or pictures are arranged on a page.
Letterer	A person who writes the text in the speech balloons, and effects like "ZAP!" and "POW!"
Panel	A single drawing with a box around it.
Penciller	A person who draws comic art on a blank page, before inking, coloring or lettering.
Splash	A large illustration that may cover two whole pages.
Spread	Two pages that face each other when you open a book.
Strip	A sequence of panels making up a comic.
Tier	A row of panels.